Underground Homes

Julie Haydon

Chapter 1

People

My name is Hayley, and this is my scrapbook about underground homes.

I live in a town called Coober Pedy in Australia. It can be very hot here, so many of the buildings in town are underground.

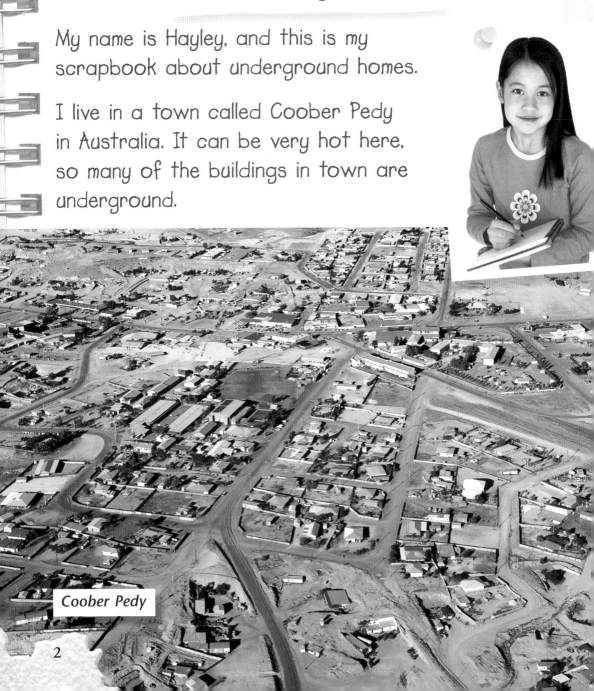

Coober Pedy

This is a photograph of my home. My home is underground. My home stays cool even on the hottest days.

Chapter 2

Earthworms

Earthworms make **burrows** in soil. Earthworms stay hidden in their burrows during the day. They come out at night to find food.

Earthworms eat dead plants, especially leaves. They pull the dead plants into their burrows to eat. Earthworms eat dirt too.

Earthworms have many enemies, such as birds. If they stay on the ground for too long, they will be eaten.

Chapter 3

Trapdoor Spiders

Trapdoor spiders dig long, thin burrows in the ground. They make a door that fits over the **entrance** to their burrow. The door is made from **silk** and dirt.

A spider can open the door to **ambush** an insect.
A spider can shut the door to keep out enemies
and bad weather.

Female trapdoor spiders lay their eggs in their
burrows.

Chapter 4

Toads

Some toads dig burrows. This toad lives in hot, dry places. It makes a burrow when there is a **drought**. It makes its burrow by digging backwards into the soil with its back feet.

In its burrow, the toad sheds some of its skin. It makes the skin into a **cocoon** that goes around its body. When rain comes, the toad comes out of its burrow to **mate**.

Chapter 5

Bats

Some bats sleep in caves during the day. They hang upside down and hold onto the roof of the cave with their strong feet. Thousands of bats often sleep together in one cave.

The bats go out at night to find food.

In winter, it can be hard for bats to find food. Many bats go into a deep sleep called **hibernation**. They wake up again in the spring.

Chapter 6

Burrowing Owls

Many owls make nests in trees. The burrowing owl lives in places where there are few trees, so it makes its home in a burrow.

The male and female owls use an old burrow made by another animal. Sometimes they will dig a burrow together. The female owl sits on the eggs in the burrow. The male owl brings her food and watches for danger.

Chapter 7

Rabbits

Some rabbits live in big groups in warrens. A warren is a large burrow. It is made up of many tunnels and rooms.

Rabbits dig many entrances to their warrens. When they are outside the warren, they listen and watch for enemies. They can run very quickly into their warren to escape from danger.

Chapter 8

Moles

This mole uses its strong front legs to dig its burrow. It pushes soil up and out of its burrow. This makes small hills on the ground. These hills are called molehills.

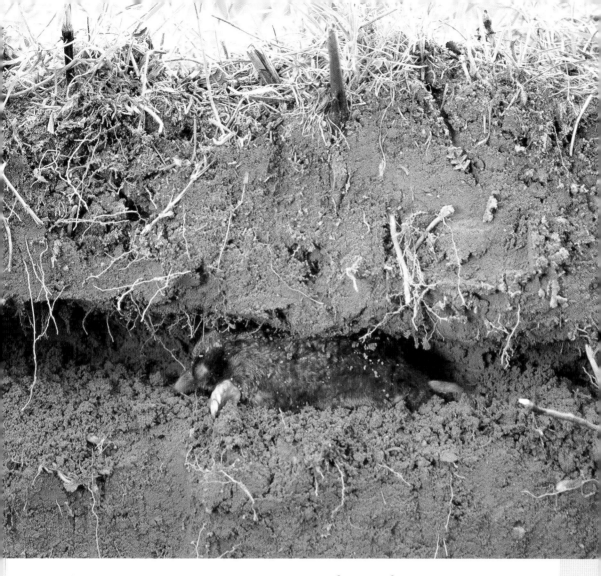

The mole cannot see well. It finds food underground by smell, touch and hearing. It eats soil animals, such as worms. When the mole finds lots of worms, it will keep the live worms in its burrow to eat later.

Chapter 9

Wombats

Wombats dig deep burrows. Burrows are often dug into the sides of hills. Sometimes the entrance to a wombat burrow is big enough for a man to crawl through.

A wombat burrow can have many tunnels. At the end of some of the tunnels are little rooms called chambers. Wombats put grass, small sticks and leaves in their sleeping chambers to lie on.

Chapter 10

Brown Bears

In winter, brown bears hibernate in dens. Dens can be in caves or in holes in the ground. The female bears give birth to their cubs in the dens. The cubs are warm and safe in their dens.

Most adult bears do not eat or drink during
hibernation. They live off the fat on their bodies.
When spring comes, the adults and cubs leave
their dens.

Chapter 11

True or False?

1. Earthworms find food during the day.

2. Trapdoor spiders make a door that fits over the entrance to their burrow.

3. Some toads live in burrows.

4. Most rabbits live alone.

5. Moles have weak front legs.

6. Adult bears do not eat or drink during hibernation.

Glossary

ambush	to attack by surprise
burrows	tunnels or holes made by animals to use as homes
cocoon	a covering an animal makes to go around its body
drought	a long time without rain
entrance	the way in
hibernation	a deep winter sleep
mate	when a male and female join together to make babies
silk	a material made inside the bodies of some animals, such as spiders

Index